DATE DUE			

CARRIE ESTÁ A LA ALTURA

Escrito por Linda Williams Aber
Ilustrado por Joy Allen
Adaptación al español por Alma B. Ramírez

Kane Press, Inc.

New York

Por Hal
—L.W.A.

Book Design/Art Direction: Roberta Pressel

Library of Congress Cataloging-in-Publication Data

Aber, Linda Williams.
    Carrie measures up!/Linda W. Aber; illustrated by Joy Allen.
    p. cm. — (Math matters.)
    Summary: Carrie measures all sorts of things to help her grandmother with her knitting projects and then Carrie decides to knit something special herself.
    ISBN 1-57565-161-0 (pbk. : alk. paper)
    [1. Measurement—Fiction. 2. Knitting—Fiction. 3. Grandmothers—Fiction.]
  I. Allen, Joy, ill. II. Title. III. Series.
  PZ7.A1613 Car 2001
  [E]—dc21
                                         00-043819
                                              CIP
                                              AC

10 9 8 7 6 5 4 3 2 1

First published in the United States of America in 2001 by Kane Press, Inc.
Printed in Hong Kong.

MATH MATTERS is a registered trademark of Kane Press Inc.

www.kanepress.com

Spiffy está dejando huellas con la nariz por toda la ventana, pero a mí no me molesta. El me está ayudando a esperar a mi Abuelita. ¡Ella viene a visitar por dos semanas completas!

Spiffy es un gran vigía. Nunca parpadea.

—Continúa mirando, Spiffy —le digo. Me pruebo algunos suéteres. Quiero ponerme uno de los que Abuelita me ha hecho, ¡pero es difícil escoger!

Abuelita es una tejedora. Ella lleva su hilo de tejer y sus agujas a cualquier lugar que va. Todos en mi familia tienen toneladas de cosas que ella ha hecho. ¡Hasta Spiffy!

De verdad deseo poder tejer como Abuelita. Ella dice que me va a enseñar algún día. No puedo esperar.

—¡Ruff, ruff, ruff! —ladra Spiffy.

—¡Llegó Abuelita! —grito. Bajo los escalones corriendo y abro la puerta.

—¡Hola, Cariño! —dice Abuelita. Ella tiene una maleta y, naturalmente, su GRANDE bolsa de tejer.

Después de todos los abrazos y saludos,
Abuelita se acomoda en su silla favorita. Ella la
llama su "silla, siéntate y teje."

—¡Tará! —dice. Entonces me da una bolsa
color púrpura, un vestido para mi muñeca
favorita, y un sombrero gracioso y alado.

—¡Todo es fantástico! —le digo.

Las agujas de tejer de Abuelita ya están sonando. —¿Me puedes dar un trabajo? —le pregunto. Me gusta ayudarle a Abuelita.

—Tú puedes ser mi espía medidora —me dice.

—¿Quieres decir que me esconda y mida cuando nadie esté mirando? —le pregunto.

—¡Correcto! —dice Abuelita—. De esa manera mis regalos serán verdaderas sorpresas. Me da una cinta de medir azul brillante.

—Necesitarás esto.

Desenrollo la cinta. —Es larga – ¡setenta y dos pulgadas! —digo—. ¿Puedo empezar a medir ahora?

La Lista de Tejer de Abuelita

Antes de que Abuelita pueda contestar, Papá
grita —¿Alguien ha visto mi otra pantufla?

Spiffy pasa corriendo – con la pantufla de
Papá.

—¡Oh, no! —dice Abuelita—. ¡Apunta
pantuflas para Papá al frente de nuestra lista
de tejer!

¡Aquí viene la espía medidora! Echo un vistazo al estudio. ¡Perfecto! Papá está leyendo. Me arrastro y mido. Once pulgadas y media. ¡Los pies de Papá miden solamente media pulgada menos que un pie! ¡Eso quiere decir que su pie es más chico que un pie!

Ser la espía medidora de Abuelita es divertido. Cuando nadie está viendo, mido todo lo que está escrito en la lista de Abuelita.

Le tomo la medida a Spiffy para calentadores de patas.

Le tomo la medida a mi hermanito para guantes pequeños de bebé.

Tomo la medida de la computadora
de Mamá para un nuevo maletín.

Mido la aldaba de la puerta.
¡Abuelita quiere hacer una
cubierta para la aldaba de la
puerta para que los toques
sean más silenciosos!

Entonces como que me entusiasmo.
Mido todo lo que está a la vista.
¡Soy una medidora
maniática!

A Mamá le encantaría una cubierta para
la tele.

¿Una bolsa para las bolas de boliche
de Papá?

Una hamaca sería buena.

¿Qué tal cortinas para la pajarera?

—¡Alto! —finalmente dice Abuelita—. Mis tejidos nunca podrían alcanzar todo lo que has medido. ¡Es tiempo de que aprendas a tejer!

¡Por fin! Estoy tan emocionada que casi no puedo hablar.

—Vamos a La Granja de Hilo —dice Abuelita.

¡Qué gran lugar! ¡Está repleto de cosas para tejer! A la hora de irnos, tengo mi propia bolsa de tejer, agujas y bolas de hilo – Rojo Cereza, Amarillo Sol y Violeta Vívido.

En casa, Abuelita me muestra dos puntadas de tejido, tejer y rizar. Parece fácil. ¡Pero no lo es! Continúo intentándolo. Poco a poco mejora mi tejido.

Abuelita siempre dice que tejer le ayuda a pensar. ¡Tiene razón! Me llega una gran idea. —Abuelita teje para todos menos para ella —le digo a Spiffy—. Así es que voy a tejer una bufanda para Abuelita. ¡Sólo falta una semana para su cumpleaños!

Desde luego, tengo que seguir la regla de
Abuelita, "Mide primero, teje después."
Espero a que Abuelita tome una siesta.
Pronto ella cierra los ojos. Su tejido cae en
su regazo. Está dormida.

Acomodo la cinta de medir alrededor del cuello de Abuelita, exactamente como debe de ir una bufanda. Parece muy corta. Desenrollo la cinta un poquito más. —Cuarenta y cinco pulgadas parece estar muy bien —le susurro a Spiffy.

Saco algo de hilo Rojo Cereza. Decido
hacer la bufanda ocho pulgadas de ancho.
Entonces desenrollo la cinta de medir a
cuarenta y cinco pulgadas – sólo para ver
cuánto tengo que hacer. "Caramba," pienso.
"¡Eso es mucho que tejer!"

Tejo por lo que parece ser mucho
tiempo. Entonces mido

¡Trabajo más duro...

y más duro!...

"No más medir," decido. "¡Solamente tejeré, tejeré, tejeré!"

Tejo mientras veo la televisión.

Tejo mientras cuido al bebé.

Tejo en el autobús rumbo a la escuela.

¡Hasta tejo mientras mi Mamá me saca
una astilla del dedo gordo del pie! ¡Ouch!

Es el día antes del cumpleaños de Abuelita. Mis dedos están muy, muy cansados. No puedo tejer mucho más.

Decido que sería mejor volver a medir la bufanda. ¡Ea! ¡Es más larga que la cinta de medir! Oh, bien. ¡Mejor más larga que más corta!

Entonces se me ocurre. ¿Cómo termino la bufanda? Esa es una cosa que Abuelita no me enseñó.

Finalmente pongo la bufanda, agujas y todo, dentro de una caja grande. ¡La envuelvo – y la amarro con la cinta de medir!

Llega el gran día. —¡Feliz
Cumpleaños, Abuelita! —digo.
    Abuelita abre la caja. Saca la
bufanda…y la saca…y la saca…

—¡Está bellísima – y tan larga. Es la bufanda más larga que jamás he visto! —dice—. Y, ¡cielos, las agujas de tejer están aún al final!

—No supe como terminarla —le explico. Abuelita me muestra exactamente que hacer.

—¡Terminada! —dice—. ¡Es una bufanda como ninguna otra bufanda en el mundo! ¡Es una bufanda hecha para dos! Vamos a dar un paseo. La quiero lucir.

Abuelita se pone la bufanda alrededor del cuello – ¡y alrededor del mío también!

—Supongo que debemos tomar un paseo muy largo —digo —, ¡para lucir una bufanda tan, tan, TAN larga!

GRÁFICA DE LA LONGITUD

Cada pieza de hilo de tejer tiene una longitud diferente

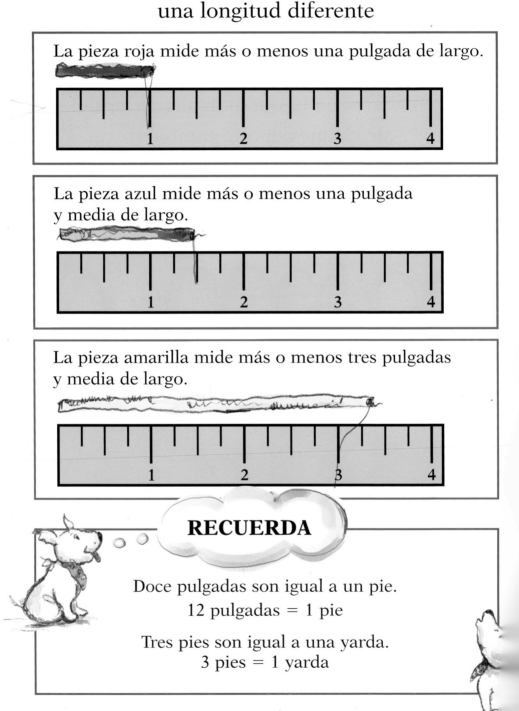

La pieza roja mide más o menos una pulgada de largo.

1 2 3 4

La pieza azul mide más o menos una pulgada y media de largo.

1 2 3 4

La pieza amarilla mide más o menos tres pulgadas y media de largo.

1 2 3 4

RECUERDA

Doce pulgadas son igual a un pie.
12 pulgadas = 1 pie

Tres pies son igual a una yarda.
3 pies = 1 yarda

EXPERIMENTS WITH ROCKS AND MINERALS

A TRUE BOOK

by

Salvatore Tocci

Children's Press®

A Division of Scholastic Inc.

New York Toronto London Auckland Sydney
Mexico City New Delhi Hong Kong
Danbury, Connecticut

This fossil fish was found in Wyoming.

Reading Consultant
Nanci R. Vargus, Ed.D
Primary Multiage Teacher
Decatur Township Schools
Indianapolis, Indiana

Science Consultant
Robert Gardner

The photo on the cover shows a collection of polished gemstones. The photo on the title page shows a section of metamorphic rock in the Sierra Nevada Mountains, Sequoia National Forest, California.

The author and publisher are not responsible for injuries or accidents that occur during or from any experiments. Experiments should be conducted in the presence of or with the help of an adult. Any instructions of the experiments that require the use of sharp, hot, or other unsafe items should be conducted by or with the help of an adult.

Library of Congress Cataloging-in-Publication Data

Tocci, Salvatore.
Experiments with rocks and minerals / Salvatore Tocci
     p.   cm. – (A True book)
  Includes bibliographical references and index.
  ISBN 0-516-22507-3 (lib. bdg.)   0-516-26995-X (pbk)
  1. Rocks—Experiments—Juvenile literature. 2. Minerals —
Experiments—Juvenile literature.[1.Rocks—Experiments. 2. Minerals
Experiments. 3.Experiments] I. Title II. Series.
QE432.2 .T62 2001
552'.078—dc21   00-069380

1 2 3 4 5 6 7 8 9 10 R 11 10 09 08 07 06 05 04 03 02

Contents

Verish sold one of the rocks known as the Los Angeles meteorite. He loaned the other rock to the Los Angeles Museum of Natural History where it is on display.

What Have You Found?

Have you ever found something valuable? In the early 1980s, Bob Verish started to collect rocks. He picked up rocks whenever he went walking near his home in California. He did this for almost twenty years. Then one day, he decided it was time to clear out his collection.

Verish came across two rocks that he had found almost twenty

5

years earlier. At that time, he did not pay much attention to them. But these rocks turned out to be very valuable. They were part of a meteorite from Mars that had landed on Earth. Only two meteorites from Mars have ever been found in the United States.

In 1866, Erasmus Jacobs also found something that turned out to be very valuable. He was helping his father on their farm in South Africa. Jacobs spotted something that he thought was a stone sparkling in the sunlight. He took it home and gave

Known as the Eureka Diamond, this was the first of many diamonds that have been found in South Africa.

it to his sister. She added it to the stones that she kept to play a game. Five years later, someone realized that the stone Jacobs found was actually a very large diamond.

The meteorite from Mars that Verish found in California is a rock. The diamond that Jacobs found in South Africa is a mineral. What is the difference between a rock and a mineral?

How Are Minerals Different from Rocks?

A mineral is a solid that contains only one substance. For example, a diamond contains only a single substance, called carbon.

There are about three thousand different types of minerals, which

The lead in a pencil is really a mineral called graphite.

come in many different colors. Some minerals, such as diamonds, are like clear glass and shine brightly in the light. Some minerals have beautiful, bright colors. Other minerals are dark and even black.

Sometimes minerals can be found lying on the ground, like the diamond Jacobs found in South Africa. Minerals can also be buried in mountains, deep inside the Earth, or even on the ocean floor. If you have ever been in an underground cave, you may have seen a mineral that forms inside the Earth. Even if you have never been in a cave, you can still see how a mineral is made.

Making a Mineral

You will need:
- two glass jars
- teaspoon
- Epsom salts
- string
- ruler
- scissors
- two small metal washers
- marker

Add water to the two jars until they are three-quarters full. Add a teaspoon of Epsom salts to each jar. Stir the water for several minutes. The Epsom salts should disappear, or dissolve, in the water.

If all the Epsom salts dissolve, add another teaspoon. Stir again for several minutes. Continue adding Epsom salts one teaspoon at a time. Stir after adding each teaspoon. Stop when you see that the Epsom salts no longer dissolve, even after you stir the mixture for several minutes.

Cut a piece of string so that it is eighteen inches long. Tie washers to both ends of the string. Place one washer in each of the jars. Place paper between the jars. Spread the jars apart so that the string hangs about one inch above the paper.

Set the two jars on a flat surface in a place where there is no draft.

Examine the string each day. White crystals should slowly start to appear on the string and grow downward. These crystals form as the water from both jars moves through the string. This water contains Epsom salts. The water evaporates from the string, but the salts remain behind. These

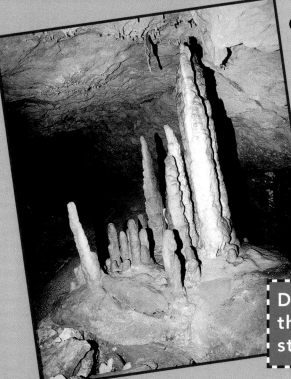

salts form crystals. These crystals may form spikes, like the stalactites that form in caves.

A mound of white crystals should also appear on the paper. Some of the water from the string drips onto the paper. As this water evaporates, salts begin collecting on the paper and form crystals. These crystals may form a cone like a stalagmite that forms in a cave.

Do the crystals on the string look like stalactites?

Do the crystals on the paper look like stalagmites?

Like all minerals, the crystals on the string and on the paper are made of one substance. The name of this substance is magnesium carbonate. No matter how closely you look in the crystals you made, all you will find is magnesium carbonate.

Stalactites and stalagmites that form in caves are not made of Epsom salts. They are made from a substance called calcium carbonate. Stalactites and stalagmites are made only of calcium carbonate.

If you look closely inside a rock,

however, you would find more than one substance. To understand the difference between a mineral and a rock, think of fruits. A mineral would be like a bowl of strawberries. No matter how closely you poked around, all you would find is strawberries. Like a mineral, a bowl of strawberries contains only one substance. A rock would be like a bowl of fruit salad. If you poked around, you might find strawberries, oranges, apples, or bananas. Like a rock, a bowl of fruit salad contains more than one substance.

Long ago, this insect became trapped in sap that seeped from pine trees. The sap slowly hardened, preserving the insect as a fossil.

One of the substances in a rock may be a mineral. In fact, a rock may contain several different kinds of minerals. Besides minerals, a rock can also contain a fossil. A fossil is what remains of an animal or plant that was once alive. How does a fossil form in a rock?

Experiment 2
Making a Fossil

You will need:
- modeling clay
- paper plate
- small seashell
- petroleum jelly
- plaster of Paris
- plastic spoon
- paper cup

Put a piece of modeling clay about the size of a large brownie on a paper plate. Rub the outside of the seashell with petroleum jelly. Gently press the surface of the seashell into the clay and then slowly lift it out. Be sure that the seashell has left a clear imprint in the clay.

If you do not have a seashell, use a chicken bone, or anything with a surface that will leave a clear imprint in the clay.

Mix four spoonfuls of plaster of Paris and two spoonfuls of water in a paper cup. Pour the plaster into the imprint in the clay. Allow the plaster to harden. Carefully remove the clay from the plaster.

Both the imprint in the clay and the plaster show how fossils are made. The clay acts like soft mud in which a living thing may have made an imprint long ago. The mud may have dried and slowly hardened into a

The plaster should look like the outside of the seashell.

18

rock. If the imprint remains in the rock, it is called a mold fossil.

Sometimes materials collect in an imprint left in the mud. This is like the plaster that fills up the imprint of the seashell. Over a long time, these materials can harden into a rock. This is called a cast fossil.

Molds are used for baking cakes. Can you see how the mold fossil got its name?

A cast fossil is like a cake that gets its shape from a mold.

What Types of Rocks Can You Find?

The walls of the Grand Canyon are made of limestone. Limestone is a type of rock called sedimentary rock. Fossils are usually found in sedimentary rock. As you can tell from its name, sedimentary rock is formed by sediments.

The limestone walls of the Grand Canyon contain many fossils.

A sediment is any substance that settles to the bottom of a liquid. Sediments that can form rock include mud, sand, and clay. These sediments settle to the bottom and form layers that may harden slowly. Layers of sediment continue building up and hardening on top of one another. The layers become cemented together to form sedimentary rock.

Making Sedimentary Rock

You will need:
- empty plastic soda bottle
- scissors
- cement mix
- ruler
- plastic spoon
- sand
- two large paper cups
- plaster of Paris

Cut off the top of a plastic soda bottle. Fill the bottle halfway with water. Pour in a two-inch layer of cement mix. Do not disturb the bottle until the cement is hard.

Use a plastic spoon to mix equal parts of cement mix and sand in a paper cup. Pour the cement-sand mixture into the bottle to form a layer about one inch deep. Allow this mixture to settle and become hard.

It may take a few days for the cement to harden.

Mix equal parts of sand and plaster of Paris in another paper cup. Pour this mixture into the bottle to form a layer about one inch deep. After this mixture becomes hard, pour off any water that remains. The hard material inside the bottle is like layers of sedimentary rock.

If a rock contains layers like these, it is most likely sedimentary rock.

Sedimentary rock can stay around for thousands of years, like the limestone walls of the Grand Canyon. But sedimentary rock can also turn into another kind of rock.

Experiment 4

Making Other Types of Rock

You will need:
- sugar
- zipper-lock storage bag
- crushed graham crackers
- chocolate chips
- miniature marshmallows
- cutting board
- rolling pin
- refrigerator
- small pan
- stove
- large glass jar

Pour some sugar into the bag so that it forms a layer. Then add a layer of crackers. Next add a layer of chocolate chips. Add the marshmallows to make the top layer. The layers inside the bag are like sedimentary rock. Squeeze the bag to remove any air. Seal the bag and lay it flat on a cutting board.

Do not worry if some items from one layer mix with those in another layer.

Use the rolling pin to press on the contents in the bag. Then place the bag in the sunlight for several hours. Repeat these steps again—pressing with the rolling pin and then placing the bag in sunlight. Do the contents in the bag look anything like they first did?

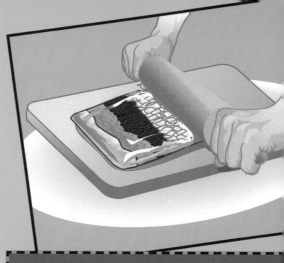

Use the rolling pin to go back and forth several times over the bag. Press the bag firmly, but not so hard that it breaks open.

Pressure from the rolling pin and heat from the sunlight changed the contents in the bag. Because of the pressure and heat, the contents of the bag are like a type of rock called metamorphic rock. Metamorphic rock is a rock that has been changed by pressure and heat.

This is an example of a metamorphic rock.

Metamorphic rocks usually form deep inside Earth, where the pressure and heat are extremely high. Sedimentary rocks that get buried deep inside Earth can turn into metamorphic rocks.

Open the bag. Put the contents in a small pan. Ask an adult to heat the contents on a stove until they melt. Then ask the adult to pour the liquid into the glass jar. The contents in the jar show what happens to substances deep inside the Earth. The substances melt because of the very high pressure and heat.

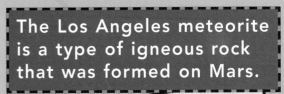

The Los Angeles meteorite is a type of igneous rock that was formed on Mars.

When the contents of the jar have cooled, place the jar in a refrigerator overnight. The next day, describe what you see in the jar. The contents in the jar are like a type of rock called igneous rock.

Igneous rock is made as melt-ed substances cool. Inside the Earth, these melted substances are called magma. If the magma cools beneath Earth's surface, it becomes igneous rock. The hot magma can also come to Earth's surface when a volcano erupts. The magma is now called lava. As the lava cools, it becomes igneous rock on Earth's surface.

Deciding if a rock is sedimen-tary, metamorphic, or igneous is not always simple. However, you can easily find out if a rock con-tains limestone.

Experiment 5

Testing for Limestone

You will need:
- marker
- three glass jars
- kitchen scale
- white chalk
- pencil
- paper
- small stones (available near your house)
- marble chips (available in a garden shop)
- vinegar
- paper towels

Use the marker to label one jar A. Label the second jar B. Label the third jar C. Weigh a piece of chalk. Write down its weight and place the chalk in the jar labeled A. Weigh ten small stones, write down their weight, and place them in the glass jar labeled B. Do the same with ten marble chips and place them in the jar labeled C. Fill the jars with vinegar.

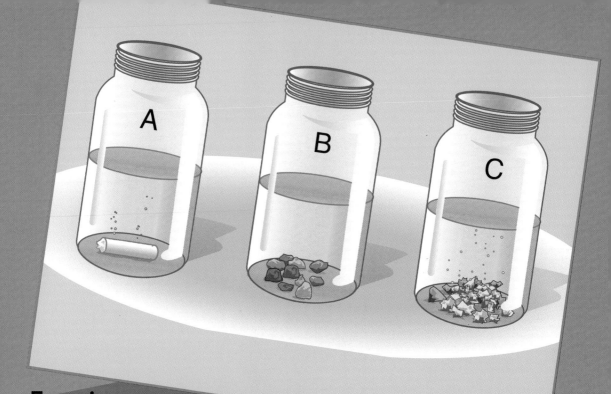

Examine the jars. Make a note of what you see in each jar.

Look closely for tiny bubbles that will start to appear in some of the jars.

The next day, pour off the vinegar from jar A. If there is any chalk left, shake it onto a paper towel. Do the same with jars B and C. Allow the chalk, stones, and chips to dry overnight. The next day weigh the contents of each jar. Do they weigh the same as they first did?

Rainwater can be an acid. Acid rain can cause statues made of marble to crumble.

Vinegar contains a chemical that is an acid. The acid gives vinegar its sour taste. In an acid, limestone slowly wears away and makes tiny gas bubbles.

White chalk and marble chips contain limestone. The limestone in the chalk and chips should wear away in the vinegar. This is why the chalk and chips should weigh less the next day. Did your stones contain limestone? If they did, they, too, should weigh less than they did when you started the experiment.

You have learned that rocks are an important source of fossils. Rocks are

Granite, which is a type of igneous rock, was used to build these pyramids, which have stood for thousands of years.

also an important source of materials used for building structures. Do minerals have any important uses?

Why Are Minerals Important?

To some people, certain minerals are considered very important. These minerals are among the most valuable things to be found in nature. These minerals are known as gems. Besides diamonds, gems include emeralds, rubies, and sapphires.

Gems such as these are very valuable minerals.

To be a gem, a mineral has to sparkle or have a beautiful color to attract attention. Why do gems sparkle? How do they get their colors?

Making Different Shapes

You will need:
- marking pen
- three plastic cups
- table salt
- Epsom salts
- alum powder (available from a pharmacy)
- plastic spoon
- scissors
- aluminum foil
- pencil
- string
- ruler
- three large paper clips
- masking tape
- hand lens or pocket magnifier

Use a marking pen to label one cup table salt. Label another cup Epsom salts. Label a third cup alum. Fill the cup labeled table salt halfway with warm tap water. Then stir in a spoonful of table salt. Stir until the salt dissolves. Continue adding salt, a spoonful at a time, until you cannot dissolve any more. Wash and dry the spoon. Repeat these steps with the second cup, but this time add Epsom salts. Clean the spoon again. Stir the alum powder in the third cup until no more of it dissolves.

Cut three pieces of aluminum foil that are large enough to cover each cup. Use a pencil to poke a hole through each piece of foil. Cut three pieces of string, each about six inches long. Tie a paper clip on the end of each string. Dip one string into the cup labeled table salt.

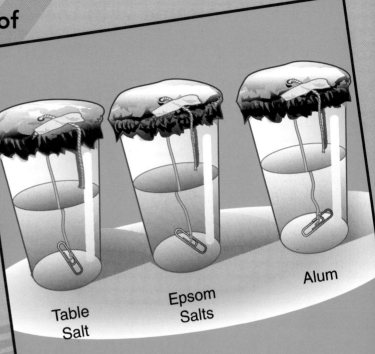

Table Salt

Epsom Salts

Alum

Place the cups in a spot where they can remained undisturbed for several weeks.

Thread the free end of this string through the hole in the aluminum foil. Place the foil on top of the cup. The paper clip should hang inside the cup. Pull up on the string so that the paper clip is just touching the bottom of the cup. Tape the free end of the string to the top of the cup.

37

Do the same with the cups labeled Epsom salts and alum. Place the cups away from any direct sunlight or heat. In about a week, crystals should appear on each string. Allow the crystals to grow for two to three weeks. Use a hand lens to examine them. Do you see that the crystals growing in each cup have different shapes?

There are more than a hundred different crystal shapes. Each shape bends and bounces light in a different way. The color and sparkle of a gem depends on the way the mineral bends and bounces light. Are minerals important for anything else besides forming gems?

Experiment 7

💡

Taking Out the Minerals

You will need:
- two glass jars with lids
- one egg
- chicken wing bone
- vinegar
- rubber kitchen gloves

Place an egg in one jar and a chicken wing bone in the other jar. Cover both the egg and chicken bone with vinegar. Screw on the lids. After several hours, remove the lid from the jar with the egg. Slowly pour the vinegar down a drain. Put on a pair of rubber gloves and carefully place the egg in your hands. How does the egg feel?

After two days, pour off the vinegar from the jar with the chicken bone and replace it with fresh vinegar. Wait another two days and then pour off the vinegar. Put on a pair of rubber gloves and hold the bone in your hands. Can you bend the bone?

Eggshells and bones are hard because they contain the mineral calcium carbonate. You learned that vinegar is an acid. Acid wears away the calcium carbonate in the eggshell. This makes the egg soft. Acid also wears away the calcium carbonate in the chicken bone. This makes the bone soft and easy to bend. Calcium carbonate is only one of about forty minerals that are important for the body to stay healthy.

Fun with Rocks and Minerals

You have learned that a mineral, such as a diamond, is made up of just one substance. A rock, such as a meteorite, is made up of more than one substance. The substances that make up rocks may be minerals. Here's a fun experiment you can do to find out something about the minerals that make up rocks.

Testing the Minerals in Rocks

You will need:
- different rocks
- fingernail
- penny
- steel fingernail file

Carry out a simple test to learn something about the minerals in rocks you pick up. Use your fingernail to try to scratch a rock. Then use the penny and the steel fingernail file to scratch the rock.

Scientists rate the hardness of minerals on a scale of 1 to 10, depending on how hard they are to scratch. The softest mineral has a hardness of 1. The hardest mineral, diamond, has a hardness of 10.

Your fingernail has a hardness of about 2.5. If you can scratch a rock with your fingernail, then the rock has a mineral with a hardness of less than 2.5.

A penny has a hardness of about 4. If a penny scratches the rock, then the rock has a mineral with a hardness of less than 4. A fingernail file has a hardness of 6.5. If the file scratches the rock, then the rock has a mineral with a hardness of less than 6.5.

Can you find a rock that has a mineral with a hardness of greater than 6.5? This rock cannot be scratched by your fingernail, penny, or fingernail file.

To Find Out More

If you would like to learn more about rocks and minerals, check out these additional resources.

 **Books**

Barrow, Lloyd H. **Adventures with Rocks and Minerals: Geology Experiments for Young People.** Enslow Publishers, 1991.

Pellant, Chris. **The Best Book of Fossils, Rocks, and Minerals.** Larousse Kingfisher Chambers, 2000.

Pough, Frederick H. Jeffrey Scovil and Roger Tory Peterson, **A Field Guide to Rocks and Minerals.** Houghton Mifflin Company, 1998.

Sofianides, Anna S. and George E. Harlow. **Gems & Crystals from the American Museum of Natural History.** Simon and Schuster, 1990.

VanCleave, Janice Pratt. **Rocks and Minerals.** John Wiley & Sons, 1996.

Wood, Robert W. **Science for Kids: 39 Easy Geology Experiments.** Scholastic, 1991.

The Children's Museum of Indianapolis
3000 North Meridian Street
Indianapolis, IN 46208-4716
317-334-3322
http://www.childrens museum.org/

This site has a section called "Geo Mysteries" under Fun On-Line where you are asked to solve mysteries about rocks, fossils, and minerals.

Geological Society of America
PO Box 9140
Boulder, CO 80301-9140
800-472-1988
http://www.geosociety.org/ educate/index.htm

Click on "Resources" for links dealing with geology, which is the study of the history and structure of Earth. One of the links gives you the opportunity to ask a geology-related question.

The Learning Web
http://www.usgs.gov/ education/othered.html

This site is maintained by the U.S. Geological Survey and has many links, including one that looks at how acid rain has affected the nation's capital.

Space.com
http://www.space.com/ scienceastronomy/solar system/moon_rock_ analysis_000522_MB_.html

Between 1969 and 1972, over 800 pounds of rocks were brought back from the moon. This site looks at some of the information that scientists have learned about the moon from examining these rocks.

Important Words

fossil preserved remains of something that was once alive

igneous rock rock formed as melted materials cool

lava melted materials on the surface of Earth that cool to form igneous rock

limestone type of sedimentary rock

magma melted materials inside Earth that may cool to form igneous rock

metamorphic rock rock that has changed because of extreme pressure and heat

mineral solid material made of a single substance that is found in nature

rock solid material made of several different substances, including various minerals

sedimentary rock rock formed from layers of sediments that harden

stalactite mineral that hangs like a spike from the ceiling of a cave

stalagmite mineral that grows into the shape of a cone on the floor of a cave

Index

Meet the Author

Salvatore Tocci is a science writer who lives in East Hampton, New York, with his wife, Patti. He was a high school biology and chemistry teacher for almost thirty years. As a teacher, he always encouraged his students to perform experiments in order to learn about science. He uses molds to make plaster casts of rocks for his HO-scale train set.